My Weirder School #9

Ms. Sue Has No Clue!

Dan Gutman

Pictures by

Jim Paillot

HARPER

An Imprint of Harper Collins*Publishers*

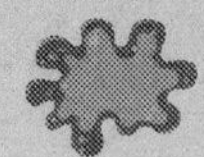

To the kids of St. Francis of Assisi School in West Des Moines, Iowa

My Weirder School #9: Ms. Sue Has No Clue!

For information address HarperCollins Children's Books, a division of HarperCollins Publishers, 10 East 53rd Street, New York, NY 10022.
www.harpercollinschildrens.com

Library of Congress Cataloging-in-Publication Data

Gutman, Dan.
Ms. Sue has no clue! / Dan Gutman ; pictures by Jim Paillot. – First edition.
pages cm. – (My weirder school ; #9)
Summary: "Alexia's mom, Ms. Sue, leads the kids of Ella Mentry School in the weirdest fund-raiser in the history of the world!"– Provided by publisher.
ISBN 978-0-06-219839-6 (hardback) – ISBN 978-0-06-219838-9 (pbk. bdg.)
[1. Fund raising–Fiction. 2. Carnivals–Fiction. 3. Schools–Fiction. 4. Humorous stories.]
I. Paillot, Jim, ill. II. Title.
PZ7.G9846Mws 2013 2013021850
[Fic]–dc23 CIP
AC

Typography by Kate Engbring
13 14 15 16 17 CG/OPM 10 9 8 7 6 5 4 3 2 1
❖
First Edition

Contents

love
GRADUAT
OVERDUE

A.J.
RYAN
MICHAEL
ANDREA
VOTE
EMILY
NEIL

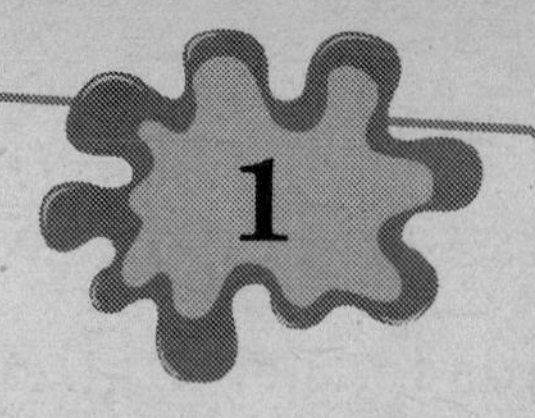

Five Thousand Dollars!

My name is A.J. and I hate dead fish.

Live fish are okay, but I don't like the dead ones.

We just finished pledging the allegiance in Mr. Granite's class when our principal, Mr. Klutz, came in. He has no hair at all. I mean *none*. But you wouldn't know it, because he was wearing a baseball cap on his head.* On the front of his cap was the word HATS.

That was weird. He was only wearing *one* hat.

"Why does your hat say 'HATS' on it?" asked my friend Michael, who never ties his shoes.

"Yeah, Mr. Klutz, do you label *all* your stuff?" asked Ryan, who will eat anything, even stuff that isn't food.

It would be weird to have a lamp with a sign on it that said LAMP. Or a table with a sign on it that said TABLE. Some stuff

---

*Where *else* would you wear a hat?

you don't need to name.

"HATS stands for Helping All to Succeed," Mr. Klutz told us. "That's what we try to do every day at Ella Mentry School."

Mr. Klutz doesn't come into our classroom very often. I figured he must have something really important to say. I hoped that we weren't in trouble. Maybe he found out what we did to Mr. Granite's pencil sharpener. Or maybe he found out what Ryan tried to flush down the toilet the other day. I tried to remember all the bad things I did recently.

"I came here to tell you children that next month is our annual school carnival," Mr. Klutz said. "I'm hoping we'll be able to raise five thousand dollars so we can buy new playground equipment."

Five thousand dollars? Is he crazy? That's almost a *million.*

"How are we ever going to raise *that* much money?" asked Neil, who we call the nude kid even though he wears clothes.

"I could sell my sister," I volunteered.

"That's illegal, Arlo!" said Andrea Young, this annoying girl with curly brown hair. She calls me by my real name because she knows I don't like it.

"Yeah!" said her crybaby friend, Emily, who agrees with everything Andrea says. "That's illegal."

"Well, maybe we can sell my sister's American Girl doll collection," I suggested. "It's worth a lot of money."

"How about we sell all these desks and chairs and school supplies?" suggested

Alexia, who rides a skateboard everywhere. “We don’t need that stuff.”

“I know,” said Ryan. “Maybe we can sell the whole *school*! It must be worth at least five thousand dollars.”

“Yeah!” all the kids agreed, except for Andrea and Emily.

Ryan should get the No Bell Prize for that idea. That’s a prize they give out to people who don’t have bells.

“If we sold the school, we wouldn’t have any place to put the playground equipment,” said Mr. Granite.

Good point.

“The reason I wanted to speak to you today,” Mr. Klutz continued, “is because

I'm looking for a parent who will volunteer to be in charge of fund-raising at the carnival."

"Fund-raising?" I asked. "What does *that* mean?"

"Well," explained Mr. Klutz, "funds are money, and raising is . . . raising."

"So you're looking for a parent who picks up money off the ground?" I asked.

Everybody laughed even though I didn't say anything funny.

"No, dumbhead," said Andrea, rolling her eyes. "Mr. Klutz is looking for a parent who knows how to raise money."

"I knew that," I lied.

"My mom used to be a professional

fund-raiser," said Alexia. "But I don't want her to volunteer."

"Why not?" asked Andrea. "I bet she would be great."

"My mom is weird," said Alexia. "She'll embarrass me if she comes to school."

"*All* parents are weird and embarrassing," I told Alexia.

"Yeah, you should see my dad," said Michael. "He trims his ear hair with a little machine that he sticks in his ear."

"*All* dads trim their ear hair," said Neil.

"All dads are weird," I pointed out. "And if our dads didn't trim their ear hair, they would have five-foot-long hair sticking out of their ears! If that's not weird, I don't

know what is."

"What about nose hair?" asked Ryan. "That's way weirder than ear hair."

"Boys are gross!" Andrea said.

Why can't a truck full of nose hair fall on Andrea's head?

We were all arguing about which was weirder, nose hair or ear hair. Mr. Klutz clapped his hands and made a peace sign with his fingers, which means "shut up."

"Alexia, is your mother's name Sue?" asked Mr. Klutz.

"Yeah . . ."

"I'm going to give her a call," Mr. Klutz said. "She could be a big help to us."

Alexia sank under her desk.

The Queen of Cupcakes

You'll never believe in a million hundred years what happened the next day. Mr. Klutz came in and told us that Alexia's mom, Ms. Sue, volunteered to do the fund-raising for the school carnival!

Or maybe you *do* believe it, because this book is called *Ms. Sue Has No Clue!* If

Ms. Sue said she *didn't* want to volunteer, the book would have a different title. Like *Miss Mitsy Is Ditsy!* Or *Mr. Putty Is Nutty!* Or *Mrs. Julia Is Peculiar!*

"Yay!" everybody yelled when Mr. Klutz told us the news.

"Boo!" said Alexia. "I'm telling you, this is a *big* mistake."

But nobody heard her, because guess who walked into the door at that moment?

Nobody! It would hurt if you walked into a door. But you'll never believe who walked into the *doorway.*

It was Alexia's mom, Ms. Sue!

Alexia hid under her desk so her mother wouldn't notice her. When your mom or dad comes into your classroom, you should always hide under your desk. That's the first rule of being a kid.

Ms. Sue was all smiles and looked very excited. She had a plate full of cupcakes in one hand. In her other hand she was lugging a giant thermometer. And I mean *giant*. That thing was taller than *she* was!

"What do you think that thermometer is for?" I whispered to Ryan, who was sitting next to me.

"I guess Alexia's mom is going to take our temperatures," Ryan whispered back.

"I can't fit that thing in my mouth," I whispered to Ryan.

"What makes you think she's going to

put it in your *mouth*?"

Ahhhhhhhh!

Ms. Sue put the giant thermometer in the corner and rested it against the wall. Then she passed out cupcakes to all of us.

"Hi boys and girls," she said while we ate. "People call me the Queen of Cup-cakes. I'm so excited to be fund-raising for the school carnival. We're going to have lots of fun and raise lots of money so we can buy new playground equipment for the school."

"Tell the children some of the great fund-raising ideas you have," said Mr. Klutz.

"Sure!" said Ms. Sue. "We're going to sell cupcakes and blah blah blah blah bingo blah blah blah blah prizes blah blah blah blah car wash blah blah blah blah parents blah blah blah blah money blah blah blah blah pony rides blah blah blah blah blah . . ."

She went on like that for a million hundred hours. It was hard for me to pay attention to what she was saying, because all I could think about was that giant thermometer and what Ms. Sue was going to do with it.

"I think we can raise even *more* than five thousand dollars," she told us. "If we raise *ten* thousand dollars, we could buy a really nice swing set and a zip line for the playground!"

Zip lines are cool. Everybody was getting excited. But not me. I kept staring at the giant thermometer. Ms. Sue probably needed to take everyone's temperature to see if we were healthy enough to ride on the zip line we were going to buy.

"Who knows?" Ms. Sue continued. "Maybe we can raise *fifty* thousand dollars! With that much money, we could get a SMART Board for every classroom in the school."

"I could really use a SMART Board," said Mr. Granite.

"The sky's the limit!" said Ms. Sue. "If we put our minds to it and work really hard, we could raise a *hundred* thousand dollars. Or even a million!"

Ms. Sue was waving her arms around

excitedly. She had a glassy look in her eyes.

"Think of it!" she said. "We could buy an iPad for every student in the school. We could get a climbing wall and a swimming pool for the gym! We could put an ice cream machine in the lunchroom! We could buy a hot tub for the teachers' lounge!"

Alexia was still hiding under her desk. I leaned over and whispered to her. "You said your mom used to be a professional fund-raiser. How come she stopped doing that?"

"She got fired," Alexia told me. "My mom tends to go overboard."

"She falls out of boats a lot?" I asked.

"No, I mean she gets carried away," Alexia told me.

"Does she get carried away after she falls out of boats?"

"She doesn't fall out of boats!" said Alexia.

"Hey, *you're* the one who said she fell out of a boat," I said. Why is everybody always talking about boats?

Anyway, Ms. Sue told us more of the great stuff we could buy with the money we were going to raise.

"We could get personal robots that carry your backpacks to school for you! We could blah blah blah blah blah blah blah blah blah blah blah blah blah blah . . ."

I wanted her to keep talking, because as long as she was talking she wouldn't be able to take our temperature with that giant thermometer. I bet the only reason why she gave us cupcakes was to distract us so we wouldn't think about the thermometer. Well, it didn't work with *me.*

Finally, Ms. Sue stopped talking. She went to the corner of the room.

It was thermometer time.

I was sweating. I thought I was gonna die.

Ms. Sue smiled as she picked up the giant thermometer.

I wanted to run away to Antarctica and go live with the penguins. This was the worst thing to happen to me since TV Turnoff Week!

"And what are you planning to do with that giant thermometer, Ms. Sue?" asked Mr. Klutz.

"This will let everybody know how much money we raise," she replied. "Every time we get a hundred dollars, we'll record it on the thermometer."

"You mean you're not going to take our temperature with that thing?" I asked.

Everybody laughed even though I didn't say anything funny.

"Of course not!" said Ms. Sue. "That would be ridiculous."

Oh. Never mind.

3

Welcome to the Carnival

Over the next month, everybody got ready for the school carnival. The parents and teachers built lots of booths and games. In art class with Ms. Hannah, we made posters. After school, we went to all the stores in town and asked if they would display our artwork in their windows. The town put up a big banner across Main Street . . .

COME TO THE ELLA MENTRY
SCHOOL CARNIVAL
ON SATURDAY!

Finally, it was the day of the carnival. When I got to school with my parents and my sister, Amy, it looked like the whole town was waiting to get into the playground. I saw Ryan, Michael, Neil, Andrea, Emily, and their parents. There were lots of balloons, and music was blasting. Booths were being set up.

One table was filled with cupcakes,

cookies, and brownies that people had baked. There was a little area for pony rides. The street next to the playground had been turned into a car wash.

Ms. Sue was running around with a bullhorn, making sure everybody was ready. The giant thermometer was mounted on a stage.

Finally, the gate to the playground opened, and we all rushed in. I could smell popcorn popping. There was electricity in the air!*

"I have a bad feeling about this," Alexia said to me as her mother climbed on the stage.

---

*Well, not really. If there had been electricity in the air, we all would have been electrocuted.

"Welcome to the Ella Mentry school carnival," announced Ms. Sue. "Before we get started, our principal, Mr. Klutz, would like to say a few words."

Mr. Klutz stepped up to a microphone and tapped it with his finger.

"Thank you all for coming out on this beautiful day," he announced. "I'm sure you're going to have a wonderful time. And just to make it extra special, I'll make a deal with you. If we raise five thousand dollars today, I will . . ."

Everybody got quiet and leaned forward to hear what Mr. Klutz was going to say. He's always making deals with us. One time he said that if we read a million

5000
4000
3000
2000
1000

pages, he would turn the gym into a video game arcade. Another time he said that if we did a million math problems, he would kiss a pig on the lips. He also married a turkey after we made a really nice Thanksgiving display. That was cool.

"If you raise five thousand dollars today," said Mr. Klutz, "I will spend a night . . . in *jail*!"

WHAT?!

Principal Klutz was willing to spend a night in jail if we raised five thousand dollars? I would pay to see *that*.

Ms. Sue walked around with a big bucket. Parents were pulling out their wallets and putting money into the bucket.

"Dad," I asked, "do you have five thousand dollars so we can send Mr. Klutz to jail?"

"I'll contribute *one* dollar," my dad told me, handing me a dollar bill to put in the bucket.

I walked around the carnival with my family. There was a long line of tables. Behind each one was a parent or teacher doing something to raise money. Ms. Hannah was in charge of face painting. Our lunch lady, Ms. LaGrange, was selling chocolates, summer sausages, and flavored popcorn.

There was a silent auction, where grown-ups could bid on all kinds of stuff.

You could buy gift-wrapping paper at one table. At another table, they were even selling Ella Mentry School underwear!

"Great news!" Ms. Sue shouted into her bullhorn. "We have raised our first hundred dollars!"

Everybody cheered. Ms. Sue put the money into a metal box, and then she drew a line on her giant thermometer.

Our Spanish teacher, Miss Holly, had the booth next to the thermometer. She had a big glass jar filled to the top with gum balls.

"The person who guesses how many gum balls are in the jar will win thirty dollars," Miss Holly told us. "It costs just a dollar to play."

My mom gave Miss Holly a dollar, and I wrote my guess on a piece of paper: A HUNDRED MILLION GUM BALLS. I hope I win!

At the next table was Mr. Tony, who runs the after-school program. A sign on his table said . . .

GOATING BOOTH.

"How does this work?" my dad asked Mr. Tony.

"Well, if you pay fifty dollars, I'll take the goat off your front lawn."

"There's a goat on my front lawn?!" asked my dad.

"Not yet," said Mr. Tony. "But there will be later today, after I put it there."

"You're going to put a goat on my front lawn?!" asked my dad.

"Not necessarily," Mr. Tony told him. "If you pay fifty dollars, I *won't* put the goat on your front lawn."

"I don't want a goat on our lawn!" my mom shouted. "They eat everything in sight and poop everywhere!"

"You'd better pay the fifty dollars, Dad," I suggested.

My dad didn't look happy. But he pulled out his wallet and handed Mr. Tony fifty dollars.

"Just so you know," Mr. Tony told him, "we're having a special sale today. For just forty dollars, I'll put a goat on somebody *else's* front lawn, and you get to choose which lawn I put it on."

"That's a pretty good deal, Dad," my sister said.

"Can we pay forty dollars to put a goat on Andrea's front lawn?" I asked.

"No!" said my mom. "Andrea's mother is my friend. I would never do a thing like that to her."

"What's the big deal?" I asked. "Andrea's mom could just pay fifty dollars, and Mr. Tony wouldn't put the goat on *her* front lawn either. Isn't that right?"

"Exactly," said Mr. Tony. "It's sort of like buying goat insurance."

"Where do you keep all the goats?" my dad asked him.

"Oh, I don't have any goats," replied Mr. Tony.

"If you don't have any goats, how can you

put them on *anyone's* front lawn?" I asked.

"Hmmm, that never came up," said Mr. Tony. "Most people just pay the money. So I don't need any goats."

What a scam. If you ask me, Mr. Tony is full of baloney.

Ms. Sue was walking around. "We're up to two hundred dollars!" she shouted into her bullhorn. She put the money in the money box and drew a new line on her giant thermometer.

The next booth had the words **PEACE** and **LOVE** written all over it. Our crossing guard, Mr. Louie, was standing there in a tie-dyed shirt.

"Hugs for a dollar," Mr. Louie shouted.

"Kisses for two dollars. Come buy a kiss and a hug."

"No thank you," my mom said as we passed by.

Right next to Mr. Louie's booth was another booth with Mr. Docker, our science teacher, standing behind it. He was holding a toad in his hand, and the sign over the booth said . . .

KISS A TOAD. ONE DOLLAR.

"This is an Eastern spadefoot toad," Mr. Docker told us. "It's a smooth-skinned toad that uses the hard spades on the hind feet to dig burrows in sand or loose dirt."

"Very nice," said my dad, "but I'm not paying a dollar to kiss it."

"No, you don't understand," said Mr. Docker. "You pay a dollar so you *don't* have to kiss it."

"So if I pay you a dollar, I don't have to kiss the toad?" asked my dad.

"That's right," said Mr. Docker.

"What if I kiss the toad anyway?" my dad asked.

"Then you don't have to pay a dollar."

"Hmm, that sounds like a fair deal to me," Dad said. And then he leaned over and kissed the toad.

Ugh, disgusting! My dad just kissed a toad! I thought I was gonna throw up.

"How about the rest of the family?" Mr. Docker asked. "Would you like to kiss the toad?"

Kiss A Toad

"No thank you!" said my mom.

"Yuck! Not me!" said my sister, Amy.

"Count me out," I said. "I'm not kissing a toad."

"Okay, that will be three dollars, please," said Mr. Docker.

My dad pulled out the money.

"Hey, you saved a dollar, Dad!" I told him.

At the next booth, there was a big tub of water with some watermelons in it. Our gifted and talented teacher, Ms. Coco, was behind the booth. The sign said BOBBING FOR WATERMELONS.

"Isn't that supposed to be bobbing for *apples*?" my mom asked Ms. Coco.

“The supermarket didn’t have any apples today,” Ms. Coco said. “So I got watermelons instead.”

“I can’t fit a watermelon in my mouth!” said my mom.

“Then you have to pay a dollar,” said Ms. Coco.

My mom handed Ms. Coco a dollar.

Fund-raising is weird.

We Have a Winner!

"Five hundred dollars!" Ms. Sue yelled into her bullhorn as she put more money into the money box. "We have now raised *five hundred dollars*!"

Everybody let out a whoop, and a new line was drawn on the giant thermometer.

My parents wanted to go bid on some

boring stuff at the silent auction. My sister went running off to hang out with her friends. Dad gave me ten dollars and said I could walk around with my friends.

They weren't hard to find. There was a section of cool games for kids to play, so I ran over. Ryan, Michael, Neil, and Alexia were there. So was Little Miss I-Know-Everything and her crybaby friend, Emily.

"Let's play water balloon toss!" Ryan said.

Our speech teacher, Miss Laney, was at the water balloon toss. She was poking her face through a hole in a shower curtain with a drawing of a clown on it.

"Betcha can't hit me, A.J.!" Miss Laney yelled.

"Betcha I *can*!" I yelled back.

"Water balloon tossing is violent," said Andrea. "I don't think it's very nice to throw objects at people. It's not a good message to send to children."

"Can you possibly be more boring?" I said to Andrea as I grabbed a big purple water balloon.

"This will cost you one dollar, A.J.," Miss Laney said.

"What?!"

"It's a *fund-raiser*!" Michael told me. "The whole point of the carnival is to make money for the school."

I pulled a dollar out of my pocket and put it in the bowl on the table. Then I picked up a water balloon and chucked it at Miss Laney.

I missed.

"Ha-ha!" yelled Miss Laney. "Nah-nah-nah boo-boo! Want to try again, A.J.?"

"Yeah!" I yelled, grabbing for another water balloon.

"One dollar, please," said Miss Laney.

I put another dollar in the bowl. Then I picked up a water balloon and threw it even harder at Miss Laney.

I missed.

"Ha-ha! You stink!" Miss Laney yelled at me. Then she stuck out her tongue and made funny noises.

"Are you gonna take that, A.J.?" Neil the nude kid said.

I took another dollar out of my pocket and put it in the bowl. This time I took careful aim, threw the water balloon a little softer, and hit Miss Laney right on the nose.

Splat! The water balloon exploded, and she was soaked.

"In your face!" I yelled, and everybody cheered.

"We have a winner!" Miss Laney said as she toweled off.

"What do I win?"

Miss Laney reached under the table and came up with a plastic bag filled with water. It took me a few seconds to realize there was something else inside the bag.

"You win a goldfish!" said Miss Laney.

Goldfish are cool.

"I will name him Fishy," I said as I took the plastic bag. "Fishy T. Fish. The *T* stands for 'The.' He will be my new friend."

Something Smells Fishy

"One thousand dollars!" Ms. Sue hollered into her bullhorn. "We have now raised one *thousand* dollars!"

Everybody whooped, and a new line was drawn on the giant thermometer. Ms. Sue put more money into the money box.

Me and the gang walked around to play

some of the other games. Ryan played ring toss. Michael threw Ping-Pong balls into paper cups. We all jumped up and down in the Moon Bounce, even Fishy T. Fish.

This was the best day of my life!

We were waiting in line to play shuffleboard when I noticed that Fishy T. Fish didn't look

very good. He was floating upside down in the plastic bag.

"Dude," Neil the nude kid said, "I think your goldfish may be dead."

"What?! How can he be dead? I just got him."

"Goldfish don't live very long," said Andrea. "I read that in the encyclopedia."

"I only had him for five minutes!" I complained.

"Yeah, but you don't know how long he was alive before Miss Laney gave him to you," Michael told me.

"What do you expect, A.J.?" asked Ryan. "He's in a plastic bag. If *we* lived in plastic bags, we wouldn't live very long either.

Look at him. He can't breathe in there."

"Fish don't breathe *air*, dumbhead," said Andrea. "They use their gills to get oxygen from the water."

"So does your *face*," I told Andrea.

"Oh, snap!" said Ryan.

"Stop arguing about it!" Emily said. "Fishy is dying! We've got to *do* something!"

Sheesh! Get a grip!

"What do you want *me* to do," I asked, "give mouth-to-mouth resuscitation to a *fish*?"

"That would be gross," said Alexia.

"Giving mouth-to-mouth resuscitation to *anybody* is gross," said Michael.

"Maybe two fish could give mouth-to-mouth resuscitation to each *other*," suggested Neil.

That would be weird.

We all rushed back to Miss Laney's booth to see if she could help us. She was wiping her face with a towel. I told her what happened to Fishy T. Fish.

"You need to talk to Ms. Sue," she told me. "She bought all the prizes."

We ran all over the carnival looking for Ms. Sue. Finally, we found her.

"I wish to register a complaint," I told her. "I won this goldfish just five minutes ago."

"Is something wrong with him?" Ms. Sue asked.

"I'll tell you what's wrong with him," I told her. "He's dead."

"No, no, he's not dead," Ms. Sue said. "He's resting."*

"He's not resting," I told her. "He's *dead.*"

"Look, I think he's doing the backstroke," said Ms. Sue. "Isn't that adorable?"

"Mom!" shouted Alexia. "He's not doing the backstroke! He's dead!"

Usually, I'm very respectful to grown-ups. But Ms. Sue was getting me really mad.

"I know a dead goldfish when I see one," I told her. "And I'm looking at one right

---

*Go to YouTube and search for "Monty Python dead parrot sketch."

now. This is an *ex*-goldfish."

"Okay, okay, maybe he *is* dead," agreed Ms. Sue. "You didn't take him into the Moon Bounce, did you?"

"I want my dollar back!" I demanded.

"I'm sorry, A.J.," Ms. Sue told me. "We're

running behind on the fund-raising, and we need every dollar for the new playground equipment. But I'll tell you what I can do. I'll get you a new fish to replace Fishy. Would that be all right?"

"Well . . . okay."

"Good," Ms. Sue said. "That will cost you one dollar."

WHAT?!

6 Cowabunga!

I decided not to buy another fish from Ms. Sue. If that one died, I'd be stuck with *two* dead fish. And I hate dead fish.

Me and the gang played a few more games, and then Ms. Sue announced that we had raised two thousand dollars. We all whooped and hollered.

"Everybody come over to the soccer field," Ms. Sue shouted into her bullhorn. "It's time to play bingo!"

"I love bingo!" we all yelled.

We rushed over to the soccer field. It was weird, because there was an orange plastic fence around the field. The grass was marked off like a big checkerboard with white chalk lines.

"How do you play bingo on a soccer field?" I asked.

"Beats me," said Ryan.

Some of the parents set up drums and other musical instruments, and they started to play oldies from a million hundred years ago. That's when the most amazing thing in the history of the world happened. A truck drove up to the field, and it was pulling a trailer.

Ms. Sue opened the door of the trailer. And do you know what walked out of it?

A cow!

"This is Dr. Moo," announced Ms. Sue. "Welcome to Cow Pie Bingo!"

"I didn't know that cows ate pie," I said.

"They *don't*, dumbhead," said Andrea. "Cow pies are poops."

"Your *face* is a poop," I told Andrea.

"Oh, snap!" said Ryan.

"Here's how we play Cow Pie Bingo," said Ms. Sue. "You folks each get to buy one square of the soccer field for twenty dollars. If Dr. Moo drops a cow pie on your square, you win a hundred dollars. The rest of the money goes to the school."

It sounded like the weirdest game in the history of the world, but all the grown-ups ran over to the ticket booth like they were giving away gold or something. Even my parents bought a square of the soccer field.

"Put your money on a square, any square!" shouted Ms. Sue into the bull-horn.

"This game sounds a lot like gambling," said Little Miss Perfect. "I'm not sure that's a good message to send to children."

"Can you possibly be more boring?" I said.

"Where do you think Ms. Sue got that cow?" Michael asked.

"My mom got it from Rent-A-Cow," Alexia told him. "You can rent anything."

After all the grown-ups got their tickets, Ms. Sue brought Dr. Moo out to the middle of the soccer field.

"Let the game begin!" shouted Ms. Sue as she released the cow.

All the grown-ups started chanting and cheering for Dr. Moo to poop on their square. It was hilarious.

"Poop on number six!" somebody shouted. "I could use a hundred bucks."

"No, poop on number ten!" shouted somebody else.

"Poop on number two, Dr. Moo!"

Dr. Moo just stood there. Everyone was on pins and needles.

Well, not really. We were sitting on the bleachers. If we were on pins and needles, it would have hurt. But everyone was watching Dr. Moo. He was standing in the middle of the field eating grass. It was exciting!

Well, it was exciting for about a minute. After that, it was just a crowd of people watching a cow stand in the middle of a soccer field eating grass.

"Mooooooo," mooed Dr. Moo.

"What if Dr. Moo doesn't poop at all?" somebody yelled.

"Oh, he'll poop," Ms. Sue replied. "They fed him just before bringing him over here."

"What if he poops on a line between two squares?" somebody asked.

"I am the Official Pie Inspector," said Ms. Sue. "I will determine which square has the most cow pie on it."

Dr. Moo took a few steps, and everyone got excited again. The parents with the musical instruments started playing a song. It was a weird song. Dr. Moo stared at the sky for a few minutes. He took a step forward. Then he took a step backward. Then he chewed for a while.

"Moooooo," mooed Dr. Moo.

If you ask me, Cow Pie Bingo is the most boring game in the history of the world.

"This would be a good time for you folks to buy some lemonade and cupcakes," shouted Ms. Sue into her bullhorn.

It took about a million hundred hours, but *finally* something dropped out of Dr. Moo's behind.

"We have a cow pie sighting!" Ms. Sue shouted excitedly as she ran over to inspect it. "It landed on . . . square number twenty!"

"That's mine!" some guy shouted, jumping up and down. "I win!"

The guy got his hundred dollars, and everybody cheered as he had his picture taken with Dr. Moo.

Ms. Sue told us that Cow Pie Bingo had raised another thousand dollars for the school. She put the money into the money box.

I looked at the giant thermometer. We were up to three thousand dollars now—more than halfway there. We needed just two thousand more dollars if we wanted to get the playground equipment and have Mr. Klutz spend a night in jail.*

---

*What are you looking down here for? The chapter is finished! Read the next one!

You Should Have Been There

"It's time for the Big Car Smash!" Ms. Sue shouted into her bullhorn.

"Car smash?" we all asked. "What's that?"

She didn't need to tell us the answer. At that moment, a tow truck came around the corner driven by our custodian, Miss

Lazar. She was towing a junky old car. Miss Lazar put the car in the corner of the playground. Then she got out of the tow truck with a sledgehammer.

"One swing for one dollar," she shouted. Then she took the sledgehammer, swung it over her head, and smashed the windshield of the car!

It was cool! Me and the guys all rushed over to get on line.

"Sorry," Ms. Sue told us. "For safety reasons, only grown-ups are allowed to participate in the car smash."

Bummer in the summer!

Smashing stuff up with a sledgehammer is cool. I can't wait until I'm old enough to smash stuff up with a sledgehammer. I will do that all day long. If you ask me, they should have a whole TV channel devoted to smashing stuff up with sledgehammers.

"Why would anyone want to damage a car on purpose?" asked Andrea.

"Because it's *fun*!" all the guys told her.

"I don't approve of violence," she said.

"What do you have against violins?" I asked. Andrea rolled her eyes.

Just about all the dads—and a few moms—paid for a turn to hit the car with the sledgehammer. A few of them hit it over and over again. By the time they were finished, there was hardly anything

left of the car. It was cool.

"It's time to play Toilet Seat Toss!" Ms. Sue shouted into her bullhorn.

Toilet Seat Toss is a lot like horseshoes,

except that you toss toilet seats. So it has the perfect name. Instead of metal stakes in the ground, there were toilet bowl plungers. It cost a dollar to toss a toilet seat; and if you got a ringer, you would win a plastic bag with a goldfish in it.

I decided not to play that game.

"It's time for the beauty pageant!" Ms. Sue shouted into her bullhorn.

Everybody came rushing over to the stage. There was a curtain across the front so we could only see the contestants' high-heeled shoes. Ms. Sue asked everybody to donate a dollar to sponsor one of the contestants. Me and the gang pushed our way to the front so we would get a good view.

"I don't like beauty pageants," Andrea said. "Beauty pageants disrespect women."

"I agree," said Emily, who always agrees with everything Andrea says.

"That's good," Ms. Sue announced, "because there are no women in this beauty pageant."

She pulled opened the curtain. Guess who was standing there?

Mr. Docker, Mr. Loring, Mr. Macky, Mr. Louie, Mr. Granite, Dr. Brad, Mr. Tony, and Mr. Harrison! And they were all wearing bathing suits and high heels!

"Aren't they lovely?" asked Ms. Sue.

The men paraded up and down the stage while this song "Isn't She Lovely" played.

Everybody was laughing their heads off. I thought I was gonna pee in my pants.

Ms. Sue had us clap our hands really loud to decide which of the contestants

was the most beautiful. The loudest applause was for Mr. Tony, so he won. I think it was because he has the most hair on his back. Ms. Sue put a crown on his head.

It was hilarious. And we got to see it live and in person. You should have been there!

After that, we all went over to the soccer field again, where Ms. Sue had set up a giant catapult that shot pumpkins across the field. People paid a dollar to shoot a pumpkin. Then we went into the gym and watched a game of donkey basketball. Yeah, with real donkeys!

There was also a dunk tank, a Dress Your Pet contest, a teacher tug of war, a mud-wrestling contest for parents, and a bug-eating contest. I went to all of them and spent almost all the money my parents had given me. I only had one dollar left.

The line on the giant thermometer kept getting higher and higher.

"We have now raised . . . four thousand dollars!" Ms. Sue shouted into her bull-horn.

Everybody went crazy.

8

Getting Desperate

Four thousand dollars seemed like a lot of money to me. But it wasn't enough. We were still a thousand dollars short of our goal, and we were running out of time. It was getting late in the afternoon. People were starting to leave the carnival. It didn't look like we were going to make it.

If we didn't reach five thousand dollars, there would be no new playground equipment. Mr. Klutz would not be spending a night in jail. Bummer in the summer!

"Don't go home, people!" Ms. Sue shouted into her bullhorn. "You need to buy a piece of duct tape first."

"Why should we buy a piece of duct tape?" somebody asked.

"So we can duct tape Mr. Klutz to the wall," Ms. Sue replied.

"Huh? What?" asked Mr. Klutz.

Ms. Sue grabbed a roll of duct tape and announced that for a dollar anyone could buy a piece and use it to tape Mr. Klutz to the wall.

"That sounds like fun," said Ryan.

"Let's do it!" said Michael.

"I always wanted to duct tape Mr. Klutz

to a wall," said Neil the nude kid.

"Uh, okay, I guess," said Mr. Klutz.

Duct taping the principal to a wall sounded like a weird idea to me. But a whole bunch of people lined up to buy a piece of duct tape. One by one, they put their tape on Mr. Klutz and attached him to the wall of the school.

Soon he was almost completely covered with duct tape. All you could see were Mr. Klutz's mouth and his bald head popping out over the top. He couldn't move. It looked like a turtle was taped to the wall. I had to admit, it was pretty hilarious.

"Now throw Nerf balls at him!" shouted Ms. Sue. "Fifty cents per throw!"

We threw Nerf balls at Mr. Klutz until none of us had any money left.

"We raised another three hundred dollars!" announced Ms. Sue. She put the money into the money box and raised the line on the giant thermometer.

But we still didn't have five thousand dollars. We were seven hundred dollars short. People put away their wallets and started packing up their stuff to go home.

"Wait!" Ms. Sue shouted into the bullhorn. "I have an announcement to make!"

Everybody stopped what they were doing. I looked at Ms. Sue. Alexia looked at Ms. Sue. Mr. Klutz, who was duct taped to the wall, looked at Ms. Sue. Everybody was looking at Ms. Sue. You could hear a pin drop.

Well, not really, because nobody brought any pins with them.

Ms. Sue reached into her purse and pulled out her checkbook.

"I'm writing a personal check for seven hundred dollars," she said.

"What?!" said Mr. Klutz. "You're going to donate your own money?"

"No," Ms. Sue replied. "The money will come out of my daughter Alexia's college fund."

WHAT?!

"Gasp!" everybody gasped.

"Mom!" yelled Alexia.

Ms. Sue wrote out a check and went over to give it to Mr. Klutz, who was still duct taped to the wall.

"Don't do it, Mom!" shouted Alexia. "I want to go to college someday!"

"I really don't think it's a good idea for you to raid Alexia's college fund," said Mr. Klutz.

"The new playground equipment will be enjoyed by hundreds of students," said Ms. Sue. "The college fund was only for one."

"But she's your daughter!" shouted Mr. Klutz.

"College isn't for everybody," said Ms. Sue.

"Your mom is weird," I whispered to Alexia.

"I told you she goes overboard," Alexia whispered back.

"She falls out of boats a lot?" I asked.

"No! I already told you! She gets carried away."

Ms. Sue wanted to put the check in Mr. Klutz's pocket, but he was covered with duct tape. So she tried to stick it in his mouth.

"No! I refuse to accept that check," said Mr. Klutz, closing his lips so she couldn't put the check in his mouth. "We don't need the playground equipment."

"Please!" Ms. Sue begged, trying to

pry his mouth open with her fingers so she could put the check in it. "Take my daughter's college fund! Don't you care about children?"

Mr. Klutz refused to open his mouth.

Well, that was that. We weren't going to reach five thousand dollars. That meant no playground equipment. No night in jail for Mr. Klutz.

Finally, Ms. Sue gave up trying to stick the check in Mr. Klutz's mouth. She ripped it into little pieces. Then she fell to her knees and began to cry. It was really sad. Alexia went over to give her a hug.

That's when the most amazing thing in the history of the world happened.

But I'm not going to tell you what it was.

Okay, okay, I'll tell you.

But you have to read the next chapter. So nah-nah-nah boo-boo on you!

A Surprise Visitor

At that moment, a long, black limousine pulled up to the playground. Everybody stopped to look at it. The door opened. A guy got out.

"Mayor Hubble!" everybody shouted.

Yes, it was Mayor Hubble. He used to be the mayor of our town. But then he got caught stealing money from people and had to go to jail.

"To what do we owe the pleasure of your company?"* asked Mr. Klutz, who was still duct taped to the wall. "I thought you were in jail."

"I got time off for good behavior," said Mayor Hubble.

Then he reached into his limo and brought out a giant piece of cardboard. It must have been the size of a surfboard.

"WOW," everybody said, which is "MOM" upside down.

"I'd like to make a small donation to the

---

*That's grown-up talk for "What are *you* doing here?"

carnival," Mayor Hubble announced. He handed the giant check to Ms. Sue. She looked like she was going to faint.

"You're giving us . . . *a thousand dollars*?" Ms. Sue said. "I . . . I don't know how to thank you, Mayor."

"No need to thank me," said Mayor Hubble. "I feel that it is very important to support our schools, and blah blah blah community blah blah blah children blah blah blah blah blah blah America . . . blah blah blah . . ."

He went on like that for a while. Everybody was crying with joy and taking pictures of Ms. Sue holding the big check. Mayor Hubble went through the crowd passing out buttons and bumper stickers, shaking hands, making peace signs, and kissing babies.

"Hooray for Mayor Hubble!" everybody started shouting. "Mayor Hubble saved the carnival!"

"How do you think he fit that check in his wallet?" I whispered to Ryan.

"He must have a *really* big wallet," Ryan whispered back.*

---

*One more chapter to go. Isn't this exciting?

10

Say It Ain't So!

Because of Ms. Sue and Mayor Hubble, the Ella Mentry School carnival was a *big* success. All together, we raised five thousand three hundred dollars. That would be *more* than enough to buy new playground equipment.

The parent volunteers started cleaning

up and taking down the booths. People started heading for their cars. That's when the most amazing thing in the history of the world happened.

A police car pulled up.

Two policemen got out. They went over to Mr. Klutz, who was still duct taped to the wall.

"Mr. Klutz," said one of the policemen, "you're under arrest. We're taking you to jail."

The other policeman cut the duct tape with a knife so Mr. Klutz could get off the wall.

"Oh yes!" Mr. Klutz said, laughing. "I almost forgot. I promised that I would spend a night in jail if we raised five thousand dollars. Well, good-bye, everybody. I'll see you bright and early on Monday."

"Monday?" said the first policeman as he slapped a pair of handcuffs on Mr. Klutz. "Don't count on it, buster. You're going away for a *long* time. We got an anonymous tip that you stole money from the school carnival."

"Gasp!" everybody gasped.

"What are you talking about?" asked Mr. Klutz. "I didn't steal any money. It's all right there in the money box. Go ahead. Open it."

Ms. Sue brought over the money box.

"How much money is in that box,

ma'am?" asked the second policeman. "Count it just to make sure."

Ms. Sue opened the money box.

"It's . . . empty!" she shouted.

"Empty?"

"Empty?!"

"Empty!"

In case you were wondering, everybody was saying "Empty."

"What happened to all the money?" somebody hollered.

"I don't have a clue!" shouted Ms. Sue.

"Okay, where's the money, Klutz?" asked the first policeman as he searched Mr. Klutz's pockets. "Where did you hide it?"

"B-but . . . but . . . ," stammered Mr. Klutz.

Me and the gang started giggling because Mr. Klutz kept saying "but," which sounds just like "butt" even though it only has one *t*.

"You have the right to remain silent," said the second policeman. "Anything you say will be used against you and blah blah blah blah."

"How could you do it, Mr. Klutz?" one of the parents

shouted. "We trusted you!"

"Say it ain't so, Mr. Klutz!" shouted one of the kids.

"You should be ashamed of yourself," shouted Ms. Sue. "Stealing money from children. You're a disgrace!"

"But I didn't do it!" Mr. Klutz protested as the cops pushed him into the backseat of the police car. "How could I have stolen the money? I was duct taped to the wall! The kids were throwing Nerf balls at me!"

"Tell it to the judge, Klutz," the first policeman said as he slammed the door shut.

"We're sending him away to the big house for a *long* time," said the second policeman as he got into the front seat.

The police car drove away.

"It must be nice to live in a big house," I said after they left.

"The big house means *jail,* dumbhead!" said Andrea, rolling her eyes.

I was going to tell Andrea that her face should be put in jail. But I didn't get the chance, because that's when the most amazing thing in the history of the world happened.

Somebody bumped into me. It was Mayor Hubble. He was walking really fast toward his limousine. After he bumped me, I turned around and looked at him.

There were dollar bills sticking out of his pockets!

I didn't know what to say. I didn't know

what to do. I had to think fast.

"It's Mayor Hubble!" I shouted. "He stole the money!"

"Get him!" somebody yelled.

Mayor Hubble started to run. He knocked over the giant thermometer. When it fell, it landed on the jar of gum balls and cracked it open!

A million hundred gum balls went rolling all over!

People were tripping over the gum balls.

Ms. Sue landed in a box full of goldfish!

Something poked a hole in the Moon Bounce, and it started deflating!

Dr. Moo got loose and rammed into the dunk tank! Water was pouring all over the place!

Everybody was freaking out!

"Run for your lives!" shouted Neil the nude kid.

MOON BOUNCE

"The ponies have escaped!" somebody shouted.

"I stepped on a toad!" yelled somebody else.

"Everyone remain calm!" hollered Ms. Sue.

While all this was happening, Mayor Hubble jumped into his limo.

"Floor it!" he yelled to his driver as he slammed the door shut behind him. The limo tore out of there with the tires squealing.

"Stop him!"

"So long, suckers!" Mayor Hubble shouted out the window.

Well, that's pretty much what happened at the school carnival. I might have added a few things just so you wouldn't get bored. It looks like we're not going to get new playground equipment after all. Maybe next year one of the other parents will be in charge of fund-raising. Maybe the police will let Mr. Klutz go and catch Mayor Hubble before he escapes with all the money. Maybe I'll sell my sister's American Girl doll collection. Maybe people will stop talking about boats all the time. Maybe the next book will be *Miss Mitsy Is Ditsy!* Maybe my dad will stop trimming his ear hair and kissing toads. Maybe we'll get personal robots to carry our backpacks. Maybe we'll get a zip line for the playground. Maybe Mr. Tony will get some goats to put on people's lawns. Maybe I'll win another goldfish. Maybe

Dr. Moo will drop another cow pie in the playground. Maybe Ms. Sue will find somebody to take Alexia's college fund.

But it won't be easy!